The Adventures of

Zoe & Alex

The Disappearing River

The Adventures of

Zoe & Alex

The Disappearing River

David Mittan and Gail Mittan

MakeThinkers

www.makethinkers.com

ISBN: 1-946125-00-8

ISBN-13: 978-1-946125-00-2

Copyright © 2016

MakeThinkers Limited Liability Company

To precious Lea and Kayla, keep your imaginations wild, your minds strong, and your hearts open. Strive for greatness. Nothing is impossible.

Acknowledgements

Thanks to our family for all their time, patience and help as we brought our first story to the world. We love you more than words can ever describe.

Thank you CC for spending hours listening to us read and reread the same sentences; your advice was golden! Thank you for believing in what we are trying to achieve. Thank you for being the kindest, most caring mother and the most supportive partner imaginable. You are truly a gem!

Thank you Jarrod, a wonderful brother & son, for being the first person to purchase the eBook and for letting our wild imagination entertain and educate your wonderful children.

Thanks Arielle for always answering our never-ending questions. You are the kind of teacher this world needs.

Thanks to Evan for always letting us ramble on whether by phone, text, email or gchat. More importantly, thanks for being a wonderful friend and one of the best, and smartest, people we know. Thanks to Fernando for the constant positive feedback – muito obrigado. Thanks to Brian for spelling his name 'Bryan' and for the totally honest feedback.

Thanks to all of our friends and family who provided thoughts, ideas, feedback or any type of positive support.

A special thanks to everyone who bought the eBook when it first launched, and to everyone who buys this book. Our world needs people like you, who care enough to make strong, creative and critical thinking children.

Thanks to all the great men and women who serve our country and keep us safe. Thanks to the educators who take the time to teach our children more than just how to beat tests. Thanks to all our editors for the hard work. Thanks to Marta for the magnificent and beautiful cover.

Think left and think right and think low and think high.
Oh, the thinks you can think up if only you try.
~Dr. Seuss~

Contents

Why We Love What We Do   i

The MakeThinkers Method   iii

    Tips for Parents Reading to Children   iv

1   The Wooden Box   1

2   The Sprites of Yellowfield   9

3   Crystal Clear Dew   17

4   Groks   25

5   The DoubleYews   33

6   Walking on Clouds   41

7   Grokland   49

8   The Chase   57

9   Wintermulligans   65

10   Home Sweet Home   73

11   A Little Bit of Extra Fun!   84

Why We Love What We Do

MakeThinkers grew out of my need to spend more quality time with my children in an impactful way. Using bedtime storytelling we were off to a good start. Its benefits were well known and widely published. Yet, it lacked that extra something. I'm sure you know about the eventual boredom that sets in with repetitive storytelling. Couldn't we use this time better? I set out to design and build a better experience.

During my time as a fellow at MIT, I began blending original storytelling with imaginative mental challenges. The goal was to combine creativity with critical thinking while forming a strong bond with my children. And, of course, short enough for me to complete in less than fifteen minutes.

I continued to experiment and tried many variations. I even asked some of my professors and friends around the world to try it out with their children. Finally, it happened! I hit the right combination.

My wife and I noticed that our family loved this new type of storytelling! Our children constantly yearned for more adventures and they were excited to solve the challenges at the end of each story! We also saw how they were beginning to mix creative thinking with logical reasoning. The way they solved problems blew our minds. On top of it all, we could also see them gaining confidence, patience, and focus. Naturally, we had a blast watching them flourish and our bond strengthened while having fun!

After experiencing this success, I had to share it with everyone. So, I started working with my mom to make it happen. She is a caring, passionate and highly accomplished elementary school educator. I grew up watching her teach and witnessing the creative ways she encouraged students to think. (Not to mention me - thanks mom!) She was a perfect fit to build out this vision.

Together we aim to take storytelling to a whole different level. We have made this entire activity straightforward and enjoyable for anyone to do. Our mission is simple: unlock the natural creativity and critical thinking skills in every child.

Through our first series, 'The Adventures of Zoe and Alex', we have put this mission into action.

We are thrilled to have you join us on this exciting journey. Get ready for a fantastic ride!

Remember, Great Parents MakeThinkers

Cheers,

David Jonathan Mittan

The MakeThinkers Method

Our stories use three steps to help children unlock their natural creativity and critical thinking skills.

Read one of the ten exciting chapters in the story.

Each chapter is designed to take under 15 minutes for parents to read to a child. It's also perfect for older kids to explore and read by themselves.

Answer the challenges at the end of each chapter.

The characters in the story need your help to solve creative and critical questions. This interactive experience develops both creativity & critical thinking.

Do the creative activities at the end of each chapter.

After reading the chapter and completing the challenges, it's now time to turn that creative and critical thinking into action. Have fun with the creative activities!

Repeat the steps until all ten chapters are complete.

Tips for Parents Reading to Children

The riddle at the end of a chapter:

Ask your children the riddle and let their minds wander as they try to solve it.

Use the clues that we provide to guide your children to the answer.

Encourage your children to provide reasons for their answers by asking them questions such as:
- Why do you think that's the answer?
- Can you think why that may, or may not, work?

The challenge question at the end of a chapter:

Ask your children the question and let them come up with different creative answers.

Encourage your children to explore other ideas by asking them questions such as:
- Are there any other ways to do it?
- Is that all, or do you have any other ideas?

Use the follow on questions to help your children critically analyze their ideas from different angles.

The creative activity at the end of the chapter:

Do the activities at your own pace and have fun!

Chapter One

The Wooden Box

Zoe opened the curtains in the attic and a reflection from the corner of the room caught her eye.

"Alex, what's that?" she asked.

She pointed to a pile of dusty old maps. Alex carefully moved the maps aside and picked up a golden colored wooden box. It was no bigger than a shoebox. There were bright blue shapes all over it — triangles, diamonds, big squares and one little circle. They had never seen anything like it before. It was magnificent!

Zoe Flynn and Alex Everhart were best friends. They both lived on Harriet Street, in a quiet, small town near New York City, where you could always find them exploring — this included many adventures in the parks, the beaches and even their own backyards. They also shared a secret that no one else in the world knew.

During the summer vacation something fantastic had happened; something that had changed their lives forever; something that had led them to spectacular new adventures.

Zoe tried to open the wooden box. Nothing happened. Alex thought maybe he could twist it open. Still nothing! It just wouldn't budge.

"What's wrong with this box? I can't find any place to open it!" said Zoe in frustration.

They looked all over the box for a keyhole or an opening and found absolutely nothing! This was very strange. Alex and Zoe handled the wooden box carefully. They didn't want to damage it, or break whatever might be inside. Could you imagine figuring out how to open the golden colored wooden box, only to find what's inside completely ruined?

2

The box reminded Zoe of an old family tale. She asked Alex if he knew the story about their great-grandmothers, Alice and Olivia, who were also best friends. Many, many years ago they had found an unusual box in the woods just a few blocks from the house.

"Yes, I've heard that one. Wasn't it a make believe story?" asked Alex curiously.

"I'm not sure," said Zoe, "but I think there was something magical in the box."

"Didn't they lose the box?" asked Alex.

"I really don't know, but I remember my mom showing me an old photograph of Alice and Olivia holding a strange looking box," said Zoe.

They stood staring at it and thinking…..

Is this the missing box? What's inside of it? How can we open it?

Alex and Zoe were in for quite the surprise if they managed to open the golden colored wooden box. They had no idea, nor could they, that inside the box were Sweaks made by the Sprites of Yellowfield. They also didn't know that the Sweaks had disappeared from the world almost 100 years ago!

All of a sudden, the window opened. Zoe and Alex stepped back completely startled. As the wind blew through the trees outside, it sounded like mysterious voices singing. They were both puzzled by the sound.

Were they hearing things? They closed their eyes and listened again. This time, paying close attention to what they heard. Yes, they were right!

The voices sang the same words over and over again:

"Gently push me down. Half of me is a smile, the other half a frown."

Zoe looked at Alex. "Did you hear that?"

"I did, but what does it mean?"

After thinking for a little bit, Zoe jumped up smiling. "The singing voices are trying to tell us how to open the box!"

"You're right!" said Alex, and he gave Zoe a high five.

The Disappearing River

Chapter One Challenge One

Solve the riddle!

"Gently push me down. Half of me is a smile, the other half a frown."

Use as many clues as you need until it's solved:

Can you list the shapes that were on the wooden box?

What does a smile look like?

What does a frown look like?

Can you put a smile and a frown together?

Chapter One Challenge Two

Zoe and Alex were lucky to find a clue to open the wooden box.

How would you open the wooden box if you weren't given any clues?

Follow on questions:

What different types of tools, devices or household items could you use to open the box?

Would they damage the box?

What questions would you ask if you found this box and wanted to open it?

Chapter One Creative Activity

Make a beautiful, magical golden colored wooden box with fancy shapes just like the Sprites of Yellowfield built for the Sweaks.

You can put a Sprite leaf inside for the Sweaks to eat!

Chapter Two

The Sprites of Yellowfield

"It's the little circle! Push it!" yelled Alex.

Zoe put her finger on the blue circle and gently pushed it in. They heard a clicking sound and the top of the box popped up. Zoe carefully took off the top and both of them stared inside speechless.

Alex reached for what looked like two pairs of eyeglasses — one silver and the other gold. As Alex touched them, a warm, tingling feeling made the hairs on his arm stand up. He gave one pair to Zoe and took the other for himself

"That's weird," said Zoe. "Why put glasses in such a beautiful box?"

Alex shrugged his shoulders.

Zoe and Alex didn't know that these weren't ordinary glasses. These were Sweaks. Wearing them let you see all the magical creatures living in hidden lands right here in our world. They were also the exact same magical glasses their great-grandmothers had found in the wooden box all those years ago.

They put on the glasses. At first everything seemed dark and blurry. Slowly, the dark faded away until they could see all around them. But, something was different. When they looked towards the open window, they now saw three fluttering figures. Alex and Zoe were amazed!

The most incredible little flying people floated in front of the window. They were about the size of a grown-up's hand and whizzed around like shooting stars. They wore shiny yellow pants and green t-shirts, with a small turquoise bag around their waist. Two of them had a bow and arrow under their wings, while the other one had a long sword. They turned and zoomed towards Alex and Zoe.

The little flying people stopped about a foot in front of their faces.

"My name is Felissa," said a little voice, "and this is my twin sister Belissa and our brother Drip. We are Sprites from Yellowfield."

Drip nodded his head and Belissa waved excitedly.

"We were friends of your great-grandmothers. We've been watching you for the past five days and singing secret —"

"Because you can't see us!" said Belissa, interrupting her sister.

Felissa gave Belissa a serious look for cutting her off. "— We've been singing secret messages to lead you to the Sweaks, the enchanted silver and gold glasses of Yellowfield. You'll need them to help us solve a serious problem that's troubling the Sprites in Yellowfield."

Alex and Zoe pinched each other to make sure this wasn't a dream.

Belissa hovered forward wearing her beaming smile.

"Hi, I'm Belissa. Did you notice a tingly feeling when you touched the glasses?"

Alex and Zoe nodded.

"Well, that's because you woke up the Sweaks and they haven't eaten in nearly 100 years! You need to feed them a Sprite leaf, or their magic will stop working and you won't be able to see us anymore!"

Felissa saw that Zoe and Alex looked confused.

"The glasses are alive," she said, "the Sprites created the Sweaks in the woods of Yellowfield using magical caterpillars, special tree branches, volcanic soil and Sprite Dew. You can feel their mouths moving behind your left ear. That's where you feed them. You must feed them immediately before they start nibbling on your ears!"

Drip felt inside his bottomless bag. He pulled out a long, thin glass vase containing one glowing Sprite Leaf.

"Ahem...This vase is under a spell to stop anyone from taking the leaf," said Drip. "You must remove the leaf without touching the vase, or the leaf, with your fingers. Or else, the leaf will turn to dust."

Chapter Two Challenge One

How many different ways can Zoe and Alex get the leaf without touching the vase?

Follow on questions:

What can they use to take out the leaf?

If the opening of the vase was very small what would you do?

What other details about the vase and leaf do you think are important to find out?

Chapter Two Challenge Two

If you had a bottomless bag, how would you find anything in it?

Follow on questions:

Which idea below is the best way to organize things in a bottomless bag? Why?

Different Ideas:

You can use long pieces of string tied to balloons.

Use Velcro to stick to the side of the bag.

Pour water into it and put everything in floating bags or containers.

Chapter Two Creative Activity

Make your own pair of Sweaks — you can decorate an old pair of glasses or make a pair out of cardboard. You can then store your Sweaks in their special box.

Don't forget to feed them Sprite leaves!

Chapter Three

Crystal Clear Dew

Alex tried to pull the leaf out of the vase using all kinds of objects: chopsticks, a piece of wire and even a long sock with chewing gum stuck to it. Nothing worked. The vase was too narrow.

Zoe stood there looking at it from different angles. She ran downstairs, returned with a bottle of water and carefully poured it into the vase. Up and up it went. They watched as the glowing Sprite Leaf floated up and out of the vase before falling onto the floor. Zoe picked it up and the Sprites zipped around in celebration!

They took turns feeding the leaf to the Sweaks and could hear them chomping away. The Sweaks let out a long sounding burp when they finished eating.

BUUUUUURP!

Zoe and Alex couldn't wait to learn more about the Sweaks, the Sprites, Yellowfield and the other incredible hidden lands in our world. Imagine being a fly on the wall listening to the Sprites speak!

Felissa flew closer to Alex and Zoe.

"In the woods, around the corner from here," she said, "hundreds of Sprites are trying to solve a huge problem affecting Yellowfield —"

"That's where we live! That's where we live!" interrupted Belissa.

Felissa rolled her eyes at Belissa.

"— In Yellowfield, there's a sparkling, clear blue river that flows into an extraordinary volcano that's no bigger than the door to this attic. A few days ago the river water mysteriously vanished."

"Like that!" said Belissa, while snapping her fingers.

Alex and Zoe giggled. They thought Belissa was very funny.

Drip then explained the importance of the river.

"The water in the river is essential for Sprites. It mixes with the red hot lava inside the volcano and turns into Sprite Dew. Early in the morning, when everyone is sound asleep, the volcano erupts and this crystal clear Sprite Dew covers all the trees and flowers around North America."

"Every continent in the world has a volcano and a magical river just like ours," said Felissa.

Zoe, who loved learning about science and nature, asked, "What happens if there's no Sprite Dew?"

"Well, the dew is what we eat. Without it, we can't fly," said Drip.

"Sprites collect it daily in teeny tiny cups. We eat what we need and store the rest," said Felissa.

"It's so delicious!" Belissa licked her lips in approval. "It tastes better than any fruit you've ever eaten! Sometimes, Drip and I fly into the huge supermarket near here to taste the yummy fruit." She had a playful grin on her face.

Alex couldn't hold back his laughter and let out a little chuckle.

Zoe said, "Hmm? So that's where those little marks on the fruit come from!"

Drip blushed and turned as red as a strawberry.

Felissa's eyes narrowed and she looked very serious. "We are not allowed near the supermarket! That's where the Wintermulligans live in the summer, and they don't like Sprites."

"Wait! You mean there are other creatures besides you?" asked Zoe.

"And, what are Wintermulligans?" asked Alex.

"More about that later," replied Drip quickly. "We must first urgently tell you about the message written on a leaf that someone left by the river."

Felissa agreed and changed the conversation to the strange message found near the volcano on the day the river disappeared.

She read the following words off a large multicolored leaf:

I don't have cards, but I have a deck,

I don't use roads, but I have a wheel,

I don't have birds, but I have a crow's nest.

I don't drink water, but I have it as a friend.

What am I?

"It's almost night time, we have to return to Yellowfield," said Drip to his sisters.

"Take some time to think about the message. We'll meet you in the attic tomorrow morning," said Felissa.

The three Sprites zoomed through the window into a setting sun.

"Bye!" yelled a bubbly Belissa, as she looped through the window.

Chapter Three Challenge One

Solve the riddle!

I don't have cards, but I have a deck,

I don't use roads, but I have a wheel,

I don't have birds, but I have a crow's nest.

I don't drink water, but I have it as a friend.

What am I?

Use as many clues as you need until it's solved:

You can walk around on my deck, but if you walk off me you'll get wet.

The wheel lets me turn left or right.

The crow's nest is up very, very high for someone to see if land is nearby.

Without water I can't go anywhere.

Chapter Three Challenge Two

How do you think the Sprites store the dew after they collect it?

Follow on questions:

Would the Sprites use special containers to prevent the dew from spilling?

How would you make containers if you lived in the woods?

Do you think the Sprites need to keep the dew hot or cold? Why?

Chapter Three Creative Activity

Build a volcano using play dough or any other materials. You can make a river flow through it just like in Yellowfield or create a volcanic Sprite Dew eruption by following the steps below.

1. Build a volcano with play dough around a cup.
2. Mix white vinegar and food coloring.
3. Carefully pour the vinegar mix into the volcano.
4. Pour baking soda onto a paper towel.
5. Roll the paper towel so it can fit into the volcano.
6. Drop it into the volcano and stand back.
7. Watch as the volcano erupts with Sprite Dew!

Chapter Four

Groks

The next morning, Zoe and Alex waited in the attic for the Sprites to arrive. When Felissa, Belissa and Drip finally flew through the window, Zoe leaped towards them.

"It's a ship! Our family has one right by the lake," she said.

The worried-looking Sprites landed on a small table in the attic.

"If that's the case, there's a good chance it's the Groks," said Felissa

"Groks?" said Zoe and Alex together.

The Groks were fierce frog pirates who lived in floating houses high up in the clouds. They were as big as pugs, but not nearly as cute, and they walked on their two hind legs. Groks, were not friends of nature. They hurt trees, flowers, rivers and even stones. They were a very selfish bunch.

"They are Color Catchers, who fly in ships and live high up in the sky," said Drip.

"What's a Color Catcher?" asked Zoe.

Drip took a deep breath. "After it rains, have you ever thought about all those different colors you see in the sky —"

"You call it... Uh, uh, uh… a rainbow!" said Belissa, interrupting her brother.

Alex nodded his head up and down very fast. He absolutely loved rainbows — art, music and science were his favorite subjects in school.

"Well, rainbows are made by the falling colors that drop from the flying Grok Ships as they soar through the sky," said Drip.

"When it rains the colors from the flowers and trees slowly wash away," said Felissa. "Sprites put little buckets in forests all over the world to catch those colors. It's our job to repaint the flowers and trees. That's how we keep Mother Nature beautiful and happy."

Belissa pulled a little black paintbrush out of her bag and swirled it around her head. A blob of red flower paint landed right on Zoe's nose. She tried to help Zoe clean it up, but her little hands spread it all over Zoe's face.

Felissa didn't even notice what was going on; thinking about the Groks had made her very angry.

"THOSE GROKS, GRRRRRRRR!" yelled Felissa. "Those Color Catchers know we stay out of the rain to protect our delicate wings. That's when they come zooming in on their ships and take our buckets of colors back to Grokland!"

She was so upset that tears welled up in her eyes. "We've set traps and even caught one or two of them, but by then it's too late. The buckets are long gone."

Belissa and Drip flew over and hugged Felissa until she felt better.

"What do they do with all the colors in the buckets?" asked Zoe, who wished she could also give Felissa a big hug.

"That's a mystery to us too," said Drip.

"Now that you know what's going on, will you come to Yellowfield and help us?" asked Belissa.

"Of course we'll help!" said Alex

"Lead the way!" said Zoe.

They followed the Sprites from the attic to the garden outside. Luckily, when you wear Sweaks they become invisible to human beings. Could you imagine trying to explain to your parents why you're wearing a pair of gold, or silver, wiggly, caterpillar glasses?

After flying down a few streets the Sprites stopped.

"Do you see those two gigantic trees ahead?" asked Felissa. "They are the powerful Oakshields of Ilan, the protectors of Yellowfield. To enter Yellowfield, you will have to answer a question."

"Good luck!" said Belissa.

The Sprites flew between the trees and vanished.

The Oakshields of Ilan greeted Zoe and Alex. In a deep voice they said together, "Only those who care about nature will be able to solve our question."

"It falls down but it never goes up," said the Oakshield on the left.

"It doesn't hurt when it falls on my toe, but without it I can't grow," said the Oakshield on the right.

Chapter Four Challenge One

Solve the riddle!

"It falls down but it never goes up,
it doesn't hurt when it falls on my toe,
but without it I can't grow."

Use as many clues as you need until it's solved:

What different objects in nature fall to the ground?

Can any of those objects break or hurt anything?

What does a tree need to grow?

Chapter Four Challenge Two

Describe how you would set up the little buckets in the woods — that catch the colors from the trees and flowers — to stop the Groks from taking them away when it rains?

Follow on Questions:

Do you think the rain could knock the buckets down or wash them away?

What would you do in case it rained so much that the buckets filled up all the way?

Does the size of the buckets — whether they are big or small — make a difference?

Chapter Four Creative Activity

Make a miniature sailing ship — similar to Phibian's flying ship — using leaves, sticks, twigs and twine.

Now see if it can float!

Chapter Five

The DoubleYews

"We know it must be something important to nature," said Zoe. "Like water, air, wind, bees or earthworms."

"Sunlight makes trees grow, but it doesn't fall down," said Alex, as he looked around for clues.

"I know something that falls down!" Zoe spun around to face the Oakshields. "The rain!"

The mighty Oakshields of Ilan stepped aside to reveal a majestic Yellowfield. Beautiful, lush green trees and dazzling, colorful flowers greeted Zoe and Alex.

It looked like a perfect summer painting you find inside The Metropolitan Museum of Art.

Yellowfield was a busy airport hub in the middle of the woods. However, instead of airplanes whizzing around, there were hundreds of Sprites with buckets and paintbrushes zooming in and out. Zoe and Alex stood on the outskirts because of their size. On the other side of Yellowfield they saw Felissa, Belissa and Drip talking to two unusually-dressed people. They had long, striped gold and white hair, and slightly pointed ears. They wore dark red, flowing cloaks and held long, bronze sticks in their hands. These bronze sticks looked similar to long hiking poles or wizard staffs.

Drip glided towards Zoe and Alex. He motioned for them to follow him. They walked around and came face to face with the two people wearing the dark red, flowing cloaks.

"This is Jack Thumperstock and Sandrabella Knight. They are DoubleYews from WizWytch," said Felissa.

"DoubleYews are the oldest living people in the world," added Drip.

Alex and Zoe introduced themselves.

"Just call me Thumperstock." He gave Alex a jolting pat on the back. "Those Sweaks are awesome! We had no idea that human beings could see us."

Sandrabella bowed her head to Zoe and Alex.

"Our job is to make sure that no creatures living in the hidden lands disturb human beings. We don't want humans asking too many questions or searching for where we live," she said. "The two of us have been flying around the world looking for our precious Cubic Rock. It was taken the other day at the Let's-Get-Along-Hidden-Creature-Convention —"

"You have to come to the conference next time," blurted out Belissa to Alex and Zoe. "There's delicious food and candy from all over the world!" She rubbed her little stomach over and over again.

They laughed at Belissa rubbing her tummy with so much energy.

Thumperstock then put his hand on Alex's shoulder and said, "WizWytch hosts a conference every second year to help build friendships across all the different hidden lands. This was the first time the Groks joined us at the conference."

Alex and Zoe tried to make sense of all this new information.

"What's a Cubic Rock?" asked Zoe.

"And, why would anyone want to take it?" added Alex.

Thumperstock couldn't believe his ears! How did they not know about the power of the Cubic Rock?

"Because, the Cubic Rock can make anything disappear and reappear," he said. "You see that huge pile of leaves over there? You can move it in two seconds to the other side of the woods using the Cubic Rock."

"Ok, ummmm... can you tell us why it's so important?" asked Alex.

"Whatever we point the Cubic Rock at disappears into the rock. We then decide when it's time to let it out. So anyone who bothers humans lands up in this rock until they learn how to behave," said Sandrabella.

Zoe and Alex were fascinated!

"What we can't figure out, is why someone took the Cubic Rock and left a message on a multicolored leaf," said Sandrabella.

"What did the message say?" asked Zoe.

Sandrabella pulled out the leaf and read the words:

I don't have wings, but I can float

I don't have eyes, but I can cry

I don't need sunscreen, but I can hide the sun

What am I?

Alex pointed to his watch. "Zoe, it's getting late. We have to go home."

"We'll think about the message later on tonight." said Zoe.

Alex and Zoe returned home for dinner and knew they had to figure this out fast!

Chapter Five Challenge One

Solve the riddle!

I don't have wings, but I can float

I don't have eyes, but I can cry

I don't need sunscreen, but I can hide the sun

What am I?

Use as many clues as you need until it's solved:

I float around and move as the wind blows.

When I turn a dark gray or black I have to let out my tears.

When there are lots of us together, we can hide the sun

Chapter Five Challenge Two

If you were extremely small, how would you move a pile of leaves in a garden?

Follow on questions:

What questions would you ask before doing anything?

Name the different things you could use to help you out with this task?

Do you think you're strong like an ant?

Chapter Five Creative Activity

Draw a picture of Yellowfield with the Oakshields of Ilan. Then glue on flowers, grass, sticks and dirt from your garden to add lively color to the picture — you can also use paint, markers and crayons.

Chapter Six

Walking On Clouds

The following day, Zoe and Alex returned to Yellowfield. They found Felissa, Belissa, Drip and the DoubleYews under a sparkling, orange-colored tree, speaking with a group of important looking Sprites. Belissa waved for them to come over.

"Hmm.....It can fly without wings," said Drip. "Well, in that case, it can't be an animal."

The Sprites and DoubleYews agreed.

"DoubleYews can fly without wings, but we have eyes, and can't block out the sun," said Sandrabella.

Belissa stretched out her hand to get Alex and Zoe's attention. She pointed to the other Sprites and covered the side of her mouth with her hand.

"This is the Council of Five. They are the Sprites who lead us….. Do you know, I've always wanted to try on one of their funky purple gowns and square hats?"

Belissa realized too late how loud she'd whispered. This time, even Felissa and Drip struggled not to laugh.

Zoe came to her rescue with an answer to the message. "Yesterday, I thought the answer might be the moon, but it doesn't cry. Today, walking over here in the shade, I realized it has to be the clouds!"

The Sprite Council of Five agreed.

"Nice work Zoe!" Belissa flew over to give Zoe the tiniest high five you have ever seen.

"It must be the Groks," said Alex. "The Groks have flying *ships* and they live in floating houses up on the *clouds*."

Thumperstock winked at Alex. "I bet they used the Cubic Rock to take the river water."

While they discussed what to do next, Yellowfield was slowly running out of Sprite Dew. There was only enough to last a few more days. The Sprites kept it fresh in a cold pebble storage dome at the mouth of the river, covered by the shade of trees, and protected by over one hundred Sprite defenders. Zoe and Alex knew they had to help recover the Cubic Rock immediately. Imagine all the trees and flowers without any color. They didn't want to see Mother Nature unhappy. Would you?

"Ok. So, what do we do now?" asked Felissa.

Crack! Zoe clapped her hands together. "It's obvious. We fly to Grokland, find the Cubic Rock, and bring it back!"

"It will have to be a small team, so they don't see us sneaking in," said Alex.

Sandrabella held her bronze stick up high. "You two can sit on the back of our flying bronze sticks."

The Council of Five gave Felissa, Belissa and Drip permission to pack their turquoise bags with enough Sprite Dew for the mission.

Obviously, Zoe and Alex had never flown like this before. They had no idea what to expect.

High up in the sky, they couldn't believe how fresh the air smelled and tasted. And, when they looked down, everything was so small that it made them feel like flying giants.

Sandrabella led them to a cloud close to Grokland. Stuck to the cloud, was a sparkling platform made by the Groks. The Groks walked on, and built houses on top of, these special platforms. It was freezing cold as Zoe and Alex walked on the cloud towards Grokland.

Whoosh! Swish! Swoosh! All of a sudden, a flying ship about the size of two cars appeared above them. A strong, fierce Grok steered the ship. They could see his short, blue spotted arms and long fingers.

He unexpectedly leaped out, landed on the cloud and stomped towards them. Felissa and Belissa pulled out their bows and Drip drew his sword. The

DoubleYews held up their bronze sticks ready to protect Alex and Zoe.

"Stop!" yelled the Grok in a deep, crackling voice. "I'm here to help! My name is Phibian Munchworth and I wrote those messages on the leaves!"

"How do we know this isn't a trap?" asked Zoe.

Alex looked cautiously at Phibian and said, "I have a plan to figure out if he's telling the truth. Where are the leaves with the messages?"

Chapter Six Challenge One

What do you think Alex plans to do in order to figure out if Phibian wrote the messages?

Follow on Questions:

Would you trust Phibian? Why?

Why do you think Phibian left the clues on leaves?

How would you have left clues for the Sprites and DoubleYews?

Chapter Six Challenge Two

If you were Zoe or Alex, how would you get to Grokland high up in the sky?

Follow on Questions:

Would the Groks hear you or see you coming?

What would you do to make sure the Groks didn't see you?

Why do you think the Groks live high up in the sky?

Chapter Six Creative Activity

Make a sparkling Grok cloud platform!

Use cotton wool to make a cloud then stick a small mirror, or aluminum foil, to the cotton wool with glue or tape.

When it's sunny outside take your new Grok platform to reflect the sun at different angles just like in Grokland. Watch how it sparkles!

(Be careful not to reflect the light at anyone's eyes.)

Chapter Seven

Grokland

Alex asked Phibian to write down a few words on his arm. Then, Zoe compared those words to the messages written on the leaves. They matched! Phibian was definitely their friend! He took quite a risk to help them. Imagine how angry the Groks would have been at Phibian if they had found those clues!

Phibian was upset and frustrated with the Groks. "I love nature. I'm so tired of living up in the clouds away from the beautiful trees and the smell of flowers. I can't pretend to be a Color Catcher anymore!"

They walked along the clouds to Phibian's ship. When everyone was safely on board, he flew the ship even higher. Alex and Zoe couldn't believe their eyes as they flew over Grokland. All the houses were round, in a bluish-gray color that reflected the sun, and they could see millions of sparkles shining on all the platforms.

Alex pointed to the bright blue sky and asked, "Phibian, what happens when there are no clouds?"

"That's a good question. We have a machine that makes clouds using heated water. It's the same type of machine that our ships use to fly, but much bigger. Look down there, you can see it."

In the middle of Grokland was a large building with part of its roof missing. A beautiful stream of rainbow colors flowed from the opening.

Phibian thought his passengers might be hungry and offered them some of the Cloudcake he had baked that morning. This cake was new to Zoe and Alex, so they first tried a small piece..... It was delicious! They loved it!

"It tastes like, *crunch crunch*, cotton candy, *crunch crunch*, chocolate, *nibble nibble nibble*, marshmallows and *crunch crunch nibble*, peanut butter," said Belissa with a mouth full of Cloudcake.

Phibian smiled from ear to ear.

"Phibian, can you tell us why Groks take our buckets?" asked Drip, as he took another bite of the Cloudcake.

Phibian told them about King Flabmore Finch and his evil plan.

"King Flabmore wants to fly like a Sprite and rule the skies! He ordered us to take your buckets from Yellowfield, collect the Sprite Dew that falls inside of them after the volcano erupts, and give it all to him."

"But, why take the entire river?" asked Felissa.

"King Flabmore has no patience. It was taking too long to collect the buckets, so he took the river to make his own Sprite Dew," said Phibian.

Sandrabella shook her head in disapproval. "How did he plan to do that?"

"He's using the cloud machine to boil the river water, like your volcano does, and to turn it into Sprite Dew. The rainbow-colored steam down there is from the water we carried up from your river. Fortunately, King Flabmore can't figure out how to get the river water out of the Cubic Rock." Phibian laughed with his deep crackling voice.

"That's something he'll never find out!" yelled Thumperstock.

"Do you know where King Flabmore has hidden the Cubic Rock?" asked Alex.

All eyes were now on Phibian. He winked with a cunning grin.

"That's exactly where I'm taking you."

The ship flew higher and higher. It continued on until it reached the highest clouds where only one round building stood. It was made of glass and reflected the color of the sky.

"It's in that building. Just don't touch it or you'll set off the alarm," warned Phibian. "I'll stay here and keep watch."

Zoe and Alex jumped out the ship and dashed towards the building. The DoubleYews and Sprites followed.

On the building, the following words were written in bright orange:

Say the answer out loud to open me.

A horsefly has one, so does a flea.

A firefly has two, what can I be?

Chapter Seven Challenge One

Solve the riddle!

Say the answer out loud to open me.

A horsefly has one, so does a flea.

A firefly has two, what can I be?

Use as many clues as you need until it's solved:

It's not what you see; listen to the words, because it's what you hear!

What can all those insects do? Say it out loud, and pronounce the consonants with emphasis!

Look at how the words are spelled in the riddle.

Chapter Seven Challenge Two

Why do you think the Groks built their houses in a round shape?

Follow on questions:

How does the wind pass or blow around objects that are round, square or triangular in shape?

If you were to build a house, what shape would you make it? Why?

What are some materials you would use to build a house?

Chapter Seven Creative Activity

What do you think cloud cake tastes like?

We happen to know that one of the secret ingredients in Phibian's cloud cake is honey.

Create and write down your own recipe for cloud cake!

Chapter Eight

The Chase

Zoe asked Alex for a marker and wrote something on her hand.

"I've got it! It's the letter 'F' from Flabmore!" she yelled.

The entire building spun around. An opening just big enough for a child suddenly appeared. They could now see a brilliant white and red light shining from the middle of the round building.

Felissa pointed at the light. "Look! There's something floating in the middle!"

"It's the Cubic Rock!" said Sandrabella.

Zoe ran to get it. Unfortunately, her arm brushed against the side of the building and set off the alarm. A loud croaking sound now filled the air.

CROOOOOAAAAK!

She grabbed the Cubic Rock, and everyone sprinted back to the ship. They saw Phibian screaming and waving his hands. Grok Ships were on their way!

Within seconds, a fleet of Grok Ships chased Phibian and his new friends. The Groks catapulted large balls of gray cloud and mud at Phibian's ship. Then, the Sprites jumped into action. Felissa and Belissa shot their magical arrows at the sails of the Grok Ships to slow them down.

Belissa fired two arrows together. "Take that and that, you Color Catchers! Not so much fun now, is it?" She stuck her tongue out at the Groks and pulled a funny face.

Phibian zipped and zoomed, flipped around in circles, turned upside down, flew left, then right and darted out of their sight. He was a brilliant flyer!

They were almost out of danger, when a ball of gray cloud and mud hit the ship's sail and sent it spiraling down towards an apple orchard next to a supermarket.

"ABANDON SHIP!" yelled Phibian.

Everyone prepared to jump out. Sandrabella and Thumperstock pulled Alex and Zoe onto their flying bronze sticks. The three Sprites grabbed Phibian and tried their best to carry him, but he slipped when another ball of cloud and mud came flying their way. Phibian fell straight through the open skylight of the supermarket.

The Sprites saw him land in a massive tub of melted, chocolate ice cream. Luckily, the supermarket was closed for electrical repairs to the open freezers and no one was around. Could you picture yourself in a store, when all of a sudden an invisible loud thump splashed ice cream all over you?

Smash! Phibian's ship crashed into the apple orchard. Zoe and Alex hid under the apple trees with Thumperstock and Sandrabella; the three Sprites stood guard. The Groks had lost sight of Phibian's ship as it went down. They flew back and forth over the orchard, searching for Phibian and the Cubic Rock.

Up in the sky, King Flabmore snarled angrily at his subjects, "We must retrieve my Rock!"

Luckily, the Grok Ships never came down low enough to see them hiding beneath the trees.

"Drip, why aren't they coming down to look for us?" asked Zoe.

"Because, we are too close to where the Wintermulligans live," he said.

"Oh no! How are we going to get Phibian out of the supermarket?" asked Alex.

Thumperstock signaled with his hands for everyone to come closer. "I've been here before on a top secret mission for the WizWytch Grand Council, follow me."

They followed Thumperstock across the orchard to the entrance of the supermarket. Zoe and Alex recognized this place. Their parents took them shopping here on the weekend. However, this was the first time they saw a small, light blue door, next to the entrance.

Alex stared curiously at the blue door. "The Sweaks are definitely still working," he said.

On the door was an odd shaped, triangular keyhole. Above it, scribbled backwards in white chalk, were the following words:

To get inside you'll need to find the Key,

So, look around and try to see,

What the next line means is where it will be:

I get bigger the more you take away.

Chapter Eight Challenge One

Solve the riddle!

To get inside you'll need to find the Key,

So, look around and try to see,

What the next line means is where it will be:

I get bigger the more you take away.

Use as many clues as you need until it's solved:

How do you play in the sand on a beach?

Have you ever played golf or miniature golf? Did you get a …. in one?

Let's go find a spade and dig!

See the chapter 'A Little Bit of Extra Fun' to find the backwards writing on the blue door!

Chapter Eight Challenge Two

Where in the supermarket should Phibian hide from the Wintermulligans?

Follow on questions:

Does Phibian's size make any difference when it comes to hiding?

Are you concerned about him leaving chocolate footprints behind?

Could he do anything to quickly erase the footprints?

Chapter Eight Creative Activity

Make your very own Cubic Rock!

Go explore in your garden and look for a see through rock. If you can't find a see through rock, look for a rock that has a unique shape.

Wash it under warm water, dry it, and paint it with similar colors to the clothes worn by the DoubleYews.

Chapter Nine

Wintermulligans

Sandrabella held out her hands and shook them. "Well, where's the key?"

"I'm not sure. It's a different clue," said Thumperstock.

Alex thought deeply about the riddle and saw Thumperstock flick up some earth with his bronze stick.

"Hey, what happens when you keep digging?" he asked with a smile.

"You make a hole…… that gets bigger and bigger the more earth you take away!" replied Zoe.

They looked around for a hole. Sandrabella found a small opening in the ground, a few feet from the door. She put her hand in it, and pulled out a piece of copper in the shape of a triangle.

"That's the key!" said Thumperstock.

He opened the door slowly and crawled inside. The others followed.

They sneaked quietly through the aisles. Thumperstock stopped just before they reached the frozen ice cream and pizza products. There stood Phibian, covered in chocolate ice-cream, surrounded by hundreds of blue haired, elf-like creatures wearing fluffy white coats.

The Wintermulligans were about the same size as Phibian. They stood in the open freezer down the middle of the aisle, and popped out of the fridge doors on both sides of it. One Wintermulligan stood high above the rest. Her beautiful, light blue eyes glared at Phibian.

"I am Queen Mirinda Agnarsson. What are you doing here Grok?" she asked in a stern voice.

Thumperstock ducked down. He spoke quietly to Alex and Zoe, "The Wintermulligans come from Greenland and need the cold to survive. It was their home for thousands of years, until the melting of the ice forced them to move. With less space to share in Greenland, the polar bears often destroyed the Wintermulligans' ice homes."

"How can polar bears see them?" asked Alex.

"Animals can see Wintermulligans and all the other living creatures in the hidden lands," said Felissa. "Did you ever see a dog barking at nothing? Well, it probably saw a Sprite, or a Grok, just like you two see us when you wear the Sweaks."

Thumperstock took another quick peek around the corner and then continued the conversation.

"The Wintermulligans travelled on ocean liners from Greenland across to New York. They landed up near the lake in the town next to where you live. In summer, their homes melt and they live in the fridges and freezers of this supermarket."

"Why don't they just stay in the supermarket all the time?" asked Zoe.

"Because they love nature and the outdoors so much," said Sandrabella.

Felissa jumped into the conversation. "Sprites have tried many times to show them how we also care for the trees and flowers. We really want to be friends with the Wintermulligans."

Belissa then pretended to throw a spear. "But, they always just throw colored ice spears at us!" she said.

The Wintermulligans were sad about moving from their beloved Greenland. They were also now scared of strangers, and were tired of rebuilding their homes every single winter.

"I have a plan to rescue Phibian," said Sandrabella. She quickly explained it to everyone.

"But, how will that work?" asked Belissa in a loud whisper.

"Shhhh! Keep it down!" said Drip.

"They'll hear us," said Felissa.

She was right! In the blink of an eye, the Wintermulligans completely surrounded the intruders. They pointed red, orange and green ice spears at them.

Belissa, recognizing the spears, wiped one with her finger and tasted it. "Yummy, they taste like the popsicles I find around swimming pools."

The Wintermulligans were not impressed.

Before anyone else moved Zoe yelled out courageously, "We can explain what we're doing here, and we can also help you with your problem!"

Chapter Nine Challenge One

How do you think Alex, Zoe, the Sprites and the DoubleYews can help the Wintermulligans?

Follow on questions:

If you were a Wintermulligan, would you like living in the supermarket freezers and fridges?

How long do you think it takes the Wintermulligans to rebuild their homes when winter starts?

Where else could the Wintermulligans live during summer? How would they get there?

Chapter Nine Challenge Two

Imagine that you are a Wintermulligan, you love nature, and you live in Greenland.

If polar bears kept destroying your home, what would you do?

Remember, you love nature, so you can't hurt animals!

Follow on questions:

Could you build your ice house in a different way to hide it from the polar bears?

What about building your ice house underground or up in a tree?

Is ice the only material you can use to build your house?

Chapter Nine Creative Activity

Design a cereal box with a funky name that you would like to find in the supermarket where the Wintermulligans live.

You can use characters from the story to decorate the box!

Chapter Ten

Home Sweet Home

"Queen Mirinda, I am Zoe Flynn and these are my friends. Please, let us tell you why we are in the Supermarket and how we can help the Wintermulligans."

"You have one minute to speak," said the Queen.

Sandrabella showed the Wintermulligans the Cubic Rock and how it worked. Using the rock, she moved pizza pies between fridges without touching them!

"The DoubleYews of WyzWytch will keep your homes safe inside our magical Cubic Rock during the summer, and return them to you when winter begins," said Sandrabella.

"That means you'll never have to rebuild your homes again!" said Felissa.

"Why should we trust you? You are friends with a Grok!" snapped Queen Mirinda. "During winter, they fly their ships near the lake and drop balls of cloud and mud on our homes!"

She crossed her arms and stared at them.

Wintermulligans were exceptionally strong. They could lift one hundred times more than a human being! The Groks knew this, and only took the Sprite buckets from the lake after dropping balls of cloud and mud that chased the Wintermulligans away.

Zoe took two deep breaths and said, "We are all lovers of nature, just like the Wintermulligans. The Grok you have is Phibian, our friend, who also loves nature."

Alex continued, "The Groks stole the Cubic Rock from WyzWytch and took the river from Yellowfield. Phibian helped us get it back."

"Your majesty," said Thumperstock, "if you look outside you'll see King Flabmore and the Grok Ships searching for us."

Queen Mirinda spoke in Mulliganese[1] to an important looking Wintermulligan near the roof. Abigail Frisk, the general of the Wintermulligan Guardians, had dark skin, bright green eyes and a fluffy coat with blue stripes. She briefly consulted with the Queen, then jumped down and headed for the light blue door followed by a small group of Guardians.

"We will help you return to Yellowfield, and you will look after our ice homes during the summer," said Queen Mirinda with a kind smile.

General Abigail and the Guardians returned to the back of the supermarket with Phibian's ship. Using their powerful strength, they fixed it, and made it even faster.

---

[1] The Wintermulligan language

Queen Mirinda, General Abigail and the Wintermulligans then said goodbye to their new friends.

"Can we please have an orange ice spear?" asked Belissa. "I'm a little bit hungry."

Queen Mirinda laughed and put one in Phibian's ship.

As Phibian took off from the parking lot, the Grok Ships tried chasing him again. This time, his ship was way too fast. He soared through the sky and left the Groks far behind. But, when they came near Yellowfield, the wind changed direction and the ship slowed down.

"What's going on with the wind?" asked Phibian.

Phibian didn't know that the Sprites had put Reversers — magical, trumpet wind blowers — high up in the trees to protect Yellowfield from the flying Grok Ships. These wind blowers only stopped working when it rained or if you whispered the daily password.

"Oh no!" said Belissa. "We never got today's password!"

Alex put his hands on his head. "What will we do if Flabmore catches up to us?"

"Don't worry!" said Drip. "Listen carefully to the wind and you'll hear it singing the clues for today's password."

Zoe heard the sweet voices in the wind and repeated the words out loud:

"They come out at night all by themselves.

And hide during the day, without going away."

Alex knew this one.

"It's the stars!" he said with a gasp of relief.

The wind changed direction and Phibian steered the ship into Yellowfield.

When they landed, Sandrabella took the Cubic Rock, held it up, and together with Thumperstock chanted, "DoubleYew, DoubleWe, DoubleMe, what's inside be set free!"

The water flowed out of the Cubic Rock and the river was back in Yellowfield. The Sprites danced in a little circle and sang merrily.

Zoe and Alex were heroes of the hidden world!

As everyone said goodbye to each other, Alex and Zoe saw tears in Phibian's eyes because he didn't have a home anymore.

"Why don't you come and live in my attic?" asked Zoe.

Alex wrapped his arm around Phibian. "We know how to feed the Sweaks, so we can always see you, and your ship can stay right outside the window.

"Does that mean I can visit my Sprite friends anytime?" asked Phibian with big, happy eyes. "That would be wonderful!"

He gave Felissa, Belissa and Drip a little hug, and said goodbye to the DoubleYews.

Zoe and Alex walked home and thought about their fantastic adventure. They wondered what other magical creatures lived in the hidden lands. One thing was certain; they would now have many, many more exciting adventures on Harriet Street.

The Disappearing River

Chapter Ten Challenge One

What other living creatures do you think Zoe and Alex might find in the hidden lands?

Parents, join our Facebook page so you can share your children's creative answers and ideas!

www.facebook.com/makethinkers

Maybe your idea will be chosen for our next story!

Chapter Ten Challenge Two

Phibian was very brave to help Alex, Zoe, the Sprites and the DoubleYews!

What can they do to make his new home in the attic a comfortable and happy place to live?

Follow on questions:

What type of house did Phibian live in up in Grokland?

Does Phibian like it to be bright or dark where he lives?

Have you thought about where he might get or make food?

Chapter Ten Creative Activity

Build a Sprite Reverser using straws and tape!

1. Tape ten straws together in a straight line.
    Make sure the tape is near the top of one side of the straws.
2. Cut the straws diagonally starting midway on the first straw from the opposite side of the tape.
3. Now gently blow through the straws or hold them up to the wind to hear the different sounds.

The Disappearing River

A Little Bit Of Extra Fun

Adventure 1: Do you think it matters that the box is made out of wood?

Adventure 2: How would you describe a bottomless bag?

Adventure 3: What special name would you give to the Sprite Dew?

Adventure 4: Why is it important for trees and flowers to have beautiful colors?

Adventure 5: Who would get tired faster: a small version of you, or a big version of you? Why?

Adventure 6: How do you think Phibian made sure the Groks didn't see him leave the messages?

Adventure 7: Which shape do you think can be found the most in a house?

Adventure 8: How would you react if you were splashed by Phibian landing in the tub of ice cream?

Adventure 9: If you had to leave Greenland, where would you go & how would you get there?

Adventure 10: Should Zoe worry that her parents might find Phibian's home in the attic?

Backwards writing on door:

'.yawa ekat uoy erom eht reggib dna reggib teg I'

eb lliw ti erehw s'taht dna snaem enil txen eht tahW

,ees ot yrt dna dnuora kool ,oS

,yek eht dnif ot deen ll'uoy edisni teg oT

We would love to hear from you!

Keep in touch with us by email;
readtome@makethinkers.com

Through our website;
www.makethinkers.com

On our Facebook page;
www.facebook.com/makethinkers

Stay posted about other wonderful books and products
by the MakeThinkers team to help your children unlock
their natural creativity and critical thinking skills.

Also available with Zoe & Alex

The Adventures of

Zoe & Alex

Holes, Moles, Snails and Slime

David Mittan and Gail Mittan

MakeThinkers

www.makethinkers.com

Chapter One

Boxes in the Attic

Alex dropped his bicycle outside the large blue and yellow house on Harriet Street. He looked up at the room with the bright green curtains.

"Zoe!" he shouted. "Are you coming down to catch some bugs?"

Zoe pushed the curtains aside and peeked through the open window. "I'll meet you in the backyard," she yelled. "I have to get the chemistry set out of the attic, so we can look at the insects under a microscope."

Zoe sprinted up the stairs to the attic, opened the door, and almost collapsed at the unexpected sight. It was completely empty except for brown boxes spread out around the room. A bead of sweat dropped down her cheek when she saw her parents packing . . . and singing. Zoe was worried that they had discovered Phibian's little round house at the back of the attic, or the wooden box with the Sweaks.

Do you remember the Sweaks? Well, Zoe and Alex shared a secret that no one else in the world knew. At the beginning of the summer, they had found a golden-colored wooden box in the attic. Inside were Sweaks made by the Sprites of Yellowfield. The Sweaks were magical glasses that let you see invisible creatures living right here in our world. Zoe and Alex had also become friends with the Sprites of Yellowfield — little flying people who keep nature colorful and beautiful, and Phibian the Grok — a frog pirate, the size of a pug that walks on two hind legs, who used to live on clouds in the sky, but who now stayed in Zoe's attic.

The MakeThinkers Team

David Mittan

David is a native South African and an avid cross-training fan. He is a voracious reader, loves learning new languages and playing chess. David holds three degrees, including an MS from UT Austin and an MBA from MIT. He is a lifelong learner with interests in finance, human health, robotics and the future of education. He's also a highly experienced investor who enjoys solving complex problems. When he isn't busy sharing MakeThinkers with parents and educators across the world, David can be found spending time with his family, playing with his two lovely daughters or strumming the guitar.

Gail Mittan

Gail is a superb elementary school educator with over 40 years of dedicated experience. She uses this extensive background to ensure that all our content is designed to maximize one goal — to help children unlock their natural creativity and powerful critical thinking skills while having fun. When she isn't busy creating delightful content with David at MakeThinkers, Gail enjoys spending time with her six grandchildren in New Jersey and continues to teach. She is also passionate about competing in walking races, crossword puzzles and gourmet cooking.

www.makethinkers.com